"The Fox (What Does the Fox Say?)"
Lyrics by Bård Ylvisåker, Vegard Ylvisåker, and Christian Løchstøer

SIMON & SCHUSTER BOOKS FOR YOUNG READERS
An imprint of Simon & Schuster Children's Publishing Division
1230 Avenue of the Americas, New York, New York 10020
Copyright © 2013 by Bård Ylvisåker, Vegard Ylvisåker, Tor Hermansen, Mikkel Eriksen,
Nicholas Boundy, and Christian Løchstøer
Originally published in Norwegian in 2013 as *Hva sier reven?*
First US edition December 2013
"The Fox" Words and Music by Bård Ylvisåker, Vegard Ylvisåker, Tor Hermansen, Mikkel Eriksen,
Nicholas Boundy, and Christian Løchstøer © 2013
Reproduced by permission of Stellar Songs Ltd./EMI April Music Inc./EMI Blackwood Music Inc.
All rights reserved, including the right of reproduction in whole or in part in any form.
SIMON & SCHUSTER BOOKS FOR YOUNG READERS is a trademark of Simon & Schuster, Inc.
For information about special discounts for bulk purchases, please contact Simon & Schuster
Special Sales at 1-866-506-1949 or business@simonandschuster.com.
The Simon & Schuster Speakers Bureau can bring authors to your live event. For more information
or to book an event, contact the Simon & Schuster Speakers Bureau at 1-866-248-3049 or visit our
website at www.simonspeakers.com.
Book design by Laurent Linn and Svein Nyhus
The text for this book is set in Joppa.
The illustrations for this book are rendered digitally.
Manufactured in the United States of America
1113 PCR
2 4 6 8 10 9 7 5 3 1
CIP data is available from the Library of Congress.
ISBN 978-1-4814-2223-9
ISBN 978-1-4814-2224-6 (eBook)

YLVIS

WHAT DOES THE FOX SAY?

Illustrated by

SVEIN NYHUS

SIMON & SCHUSTER BOOKS FOR YOUNG READERS

New York   London   Toronto   Sydney   New Delhi

Dog goes woof.

Cat goes meow.

Bird goes tweet

and mouse goes squeak.

Cow goes **moo**.

Frog goes **croak** and the elephant goes **toot**.

Ducks say quack
and fish go blub
and the seal goes OW, OW, OW.

But there is one sound
that no one knows.

What does the **fox** say?

Ring-ding-ding-ding-dingeringeding!
Gering-ding-ding-ding-dingeringeding!
Ring-ding-ding-ding-dingeringeding!

Wa-pa-pa-pa-pa-pa-pow!
Wa-pa-pa-pa-pa-pa-pow!
Wa-pa-pa-pa-pa-pa-pow!

Hatee-hatee-hatee-ho!
Hatee-hatee-hatee-ho!
Hatee-hatee-hatee-ho!

Joff-tchoff-tchoffo-tchoffo-tchoff!
Tchoff-tchoff-tchoffo-tchoffo-tchoff!
Joff-tchoff-tchoffo-tchoffo-tchoff!

What does the fox say?

Big blue eyes,
pointy nose.
Chasing mice and digging holes.

Tiny paws
up the hill.
Suddenly you're standing still.

Your fur is red.
So beautiful,
like an angel in disguise.

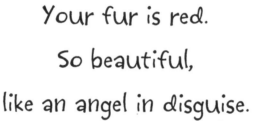

But if you meet
a friendly horse,
will you communicate by Morse?
How will you speak to that horse?

What does the **fox** say?

Jacha-chacha-chacha-chow!
Jacha-chacha-chacha-chow!
Jacha-chacha-chacha-chow!

Fraka-kaka-kaka-kaka-kow!
Fraka-kaka-kaka-kaka-kow!
Fraka-kaka-kaka-kaka-kow!

A-hee-ahee ha-hee!
A-hee-ahee ha-hee!
A-hee-ahee ha-hee!

A-oo-oo-oo-ooo!
A-oo-oo-oo-ooo!

What does the **fox** say?

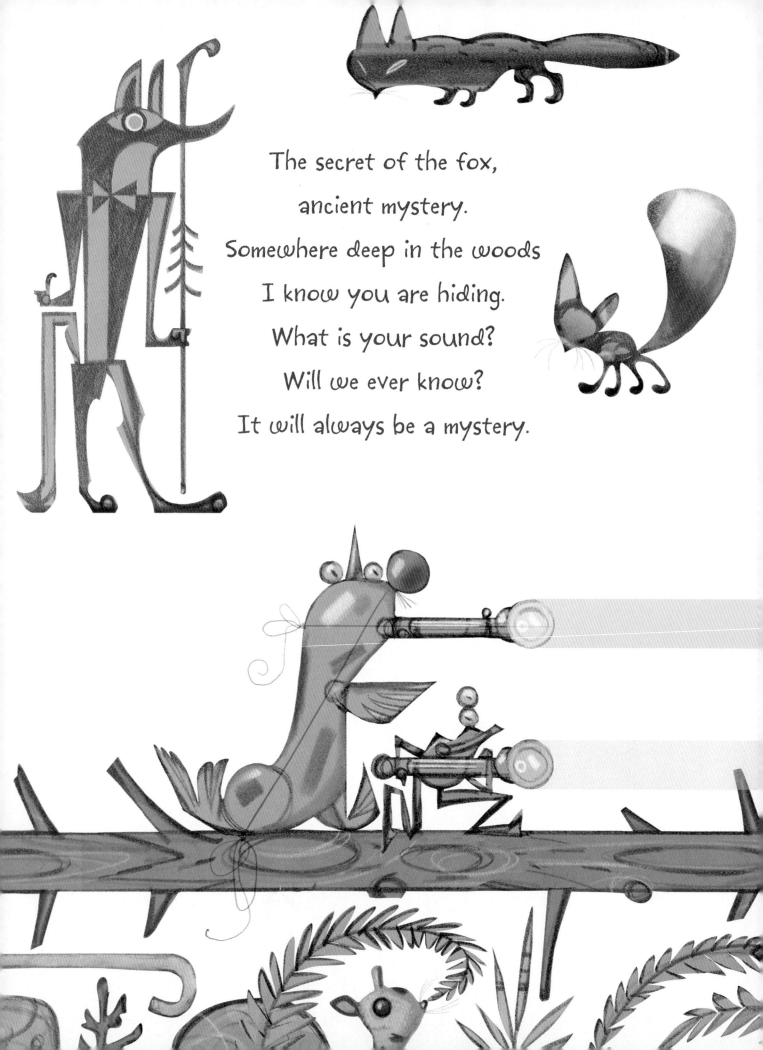

The secret of the fox,
ancient mystery.
Somewhere deep in the woods
I know you are hiding.
What is your sound?
Will we ever know?
It will always be a mystery.

What do you say?
You're my guardian angel
hiding in the woods.
What is your sound?
Will we ever know?

I want to know!

Boo-boo-bop-weydo!
Boo-dee-bee-beep-boo-beydo!
Boo-boo-bop-weydo!
Bee-bee-dee-bap-bap-weydo!
Ba-da-bap-beydo!

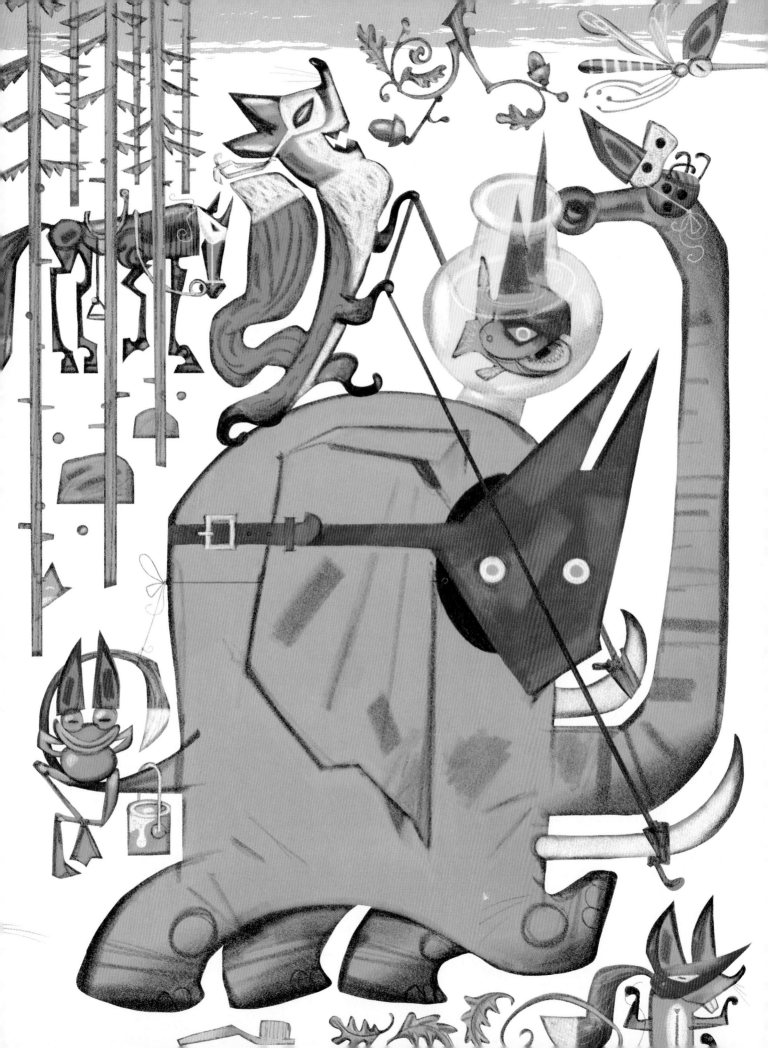